Freddie
THE FRUIT FLY

by Zane Stuart

Illustrated by Liz Sharp

DORRANCE
PUBLISHING CO
EST. 1920
PITTSBURGH, PENNSYLVANIA 15238

Dorrance Publishing Co
585 Alpha Drive
Pittsburgh, PA 15238
Visit our website at www.dorrancebookstore.com

ISBN: 978-1-6495-7123-6
eISBN: 978-1-6495-7635-4

This is Freddie. He's a fruit fly. Do you know what Freddie loves to eat?

That's right – FRUIT!

One day, Freddie was at the market, enjoying a juicy, fuzzy peach.

All of a sudden, it started to rain.

So Freddie flew to another part of the market. He flew and flew until he saw some beautiful, ripe apples. He opened his mouth to take a big bite and… OUCH! They weren't apples!

It was just a picture of apples on the label of a bottle of apple juice!

Freddie flew to another aisle. There, he saw some delicious-looking peaches. He opened his mouth to take a big bite and… OUCH! They weren't peaches!

It was just a picture of peaches on the label of a can of sliced peaches!

Freddie the fruit fly kept flying around the market until he saw a lady pushing a shopping cart. She had lots of yummy fruit in her shopping cart, including bananas, apples, peaches and tomatoes. That's right – a tomato is a fruit!

Freddie landed on the fruit. He ate some of it, and it was really good! Freddie decided to go for a ride in the lady's shopping cart. Freddie waved at the people in the market as they walked by.

When they came to the checkout counter, the lady put the fruit, with Freddie, onto the conveyor belt. The man at the counter placed the fruit, and Freddie, onto the scale and then into a paper bag.

As the lady wheeled her shopping cart to the door, Freddie thought, "I like this lady. I think I'll go home with her!"

19

The lady put her bags, and Freddie, into her car, and off they went! Freddie had never ridden in a car before. He thought it was fun!

When they arrived at the lady's house, the lady carried her bags, with Freddie, into her kitchen. She reached into the bag and put the fruit, and Freddie, into a basket on the counter. Freddie liked the lady's kitchen. Everything was nice and shiny.

Freddie watched as the nice lady made herself a cup of tea and took it to the table. Just then, Freddie heard a very pleasant buzzing. "Hi," said a very sweet voice. It was another fruit fly! Freddie was so excited, he could hardly contain himself. "Hi," said Freddie. "What's your name?" "Francine," she said, smiling her prettiest smile. "I just got here," said Freddie. "The lady brought me here from the market."

"That's nice," said Francine. "What's a market?" "That's where people buy food," said Freddie. "Oh," said Francine. "You're cute!" Freddie blushed and tried not to feel nervous. "Thanks," said Freddie. "I th-think you're c-cute, too." Freddie and Francine talked and flew and ate together all that day.

When evening came, Francine fell fast asleep, nestling in some peach leaves. Freddie slept in a hole that he had eaten into a strawberry.

In the middle of the night, they were awakened by a line of ants that were marching by on the counter. "Hey, what are you guys doing?" asked Freddie. The ant at the head of the line said, "One of our scouts found some cake crumbs that the lady left out, and we're going to get them and take them back to our nest. Sorry if we woke you." "That's okay," said Freddie. "See you later."

The ants carried away all of the crumbs, and soon they were gone. Freddie and Francine went back to sleep, and the next time they awoke, it was morning.

The lady was back in the kitchen, making herself some breakfast. Freddie and Francine had breakfast, too, enjoying some peaches and strawberries.

Suddenly, a big furry thing jumped up onto the counter. It meowed and purred, and walked right past Freddie and Francine. "What's that?" asked Freddie.

"Oh, that's just the lady's cat," said Francine. "He won't bother us. We're too little."

Just then, some fleas jumped off the cat's back and landed right next to Freddie and Francine. "Hi," said one of them. "We're fleas. We live on the cat. Who are you?" "We're fruit flies. I came here from the market," said Freddie. "I've been here as long as I can remember," said Francine.

"Well, nice to meet you," said the flea. "Gotta go – the cat's moving."

And with that, the fleas hopped back onto the cat, and away they went.

As the weeks went by, Freddie and Francine grew to be more and more fond of each other. They spent lots of time together, and they were very happy. After a while, Freddie and Francine decided to get married! They excitedly began to plan their wedding. They invited the ants and the fleas, and the fleas said that they would bring some of their friends along to play music.

Soon the big day arrived. And when the lady went out to visit some friends, the wedding began.

Join us for the

Wedding

of

Freddie & Francine

It was a lovely ceremony. It was presided over by a kind old water bug. Francine wore a beautiful gown made from some tissue paper that some pears had been wrapped in. Freddie wore a suit made from peach leaves.

After the ceremony, the party began. Everyone danced and danced to the music of The Bug Band.

As the party was ending, Freddie and Francine fell fast asleep on a banana peel that was in a basket on the floor.

While they were sleeping, the lady came home. She picked up the basket that Freddie and Francine were sleeping in and took it outside and put it by the curb – but she forgot to tie up the bag!

The next morning, there was a big rumbling sound, and Freddie and Francine found themselves in the back of a big truck, driving away on their honeymoon vacation!

The truck drove through the town until it came to a wharf at the edge of the ocean. There was another big rumbling sound, and Freddie and Francine found themselves on a big flat boat, heading out to sea on their honeymoon cruise!

They had never seen the ocean before, and they could hardly believe how big it was. As they were admiring the rolling blue water, a gust of wind suddenly came up and swept Freddie and Francine high into the sky!

They flew and flew for a long time until they saw a beautiful green island. The wind slowed down, and Freddie and Francine were able to land on the beach.

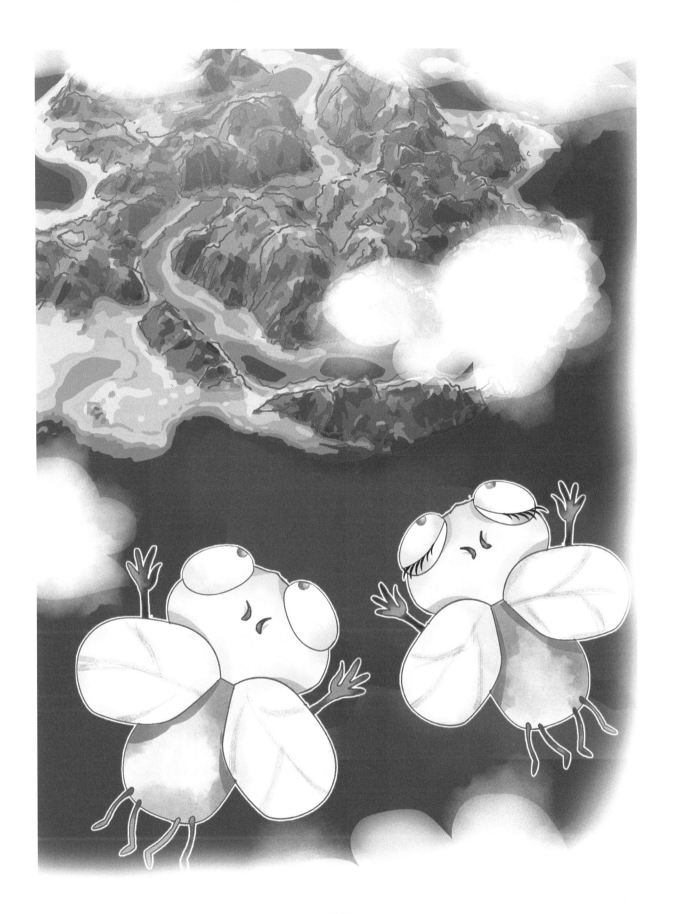

The island was just perfect! And the trees were full of tropical fruit, including bananas, mangos, papayas and breadfruit. Freddie and Francine feasted on the wonderful fruit, and they were very happy to be in such a beautiful place.

Francine said to Freddie, "Let's stay on this island, raise a big family, and live happily ever after."

"That sounds perfect!" said Freddie.

And that's exactly what they did!

The End

CPSIA information can be obtained
at www.ICGtesting.com
Printed in the USA
BVHW052357240521
606835BV00001B/3